Wendy Cheyette Lewison

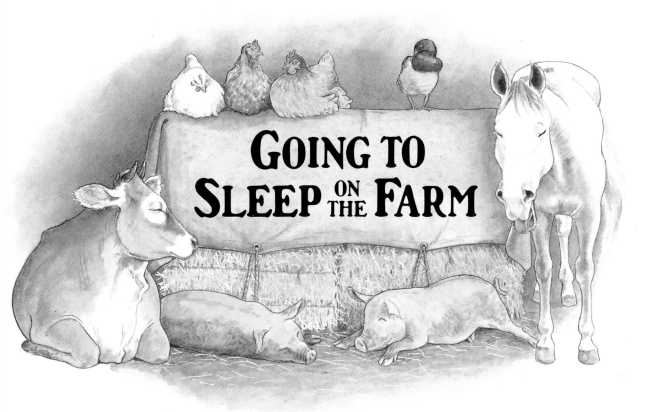

GOING TO SLEEP ON THE FARM

pictures by Juan Wijngaard

A Puffin Pied Piper

For Bea and Josh Cheyette, my mother and father,
who sang me to sleep. W.C.L.

To Patrick J.W.

PUFFIN PIED PIPER BOOKS
Published by the Penguin Group
Penguin Books USA Inc., 375 Hudson Street, New York, New York, 10014, U.S.A.
Penguin Books Ltd, 27 Wrights Lane, London W8 5TZ, England
Penguin Books Australia Ltd, Ringwood, Victoria, Australia
Penguin Books Canada Ltd, 10 Alcorn Avenue, Toronto, Ontario, Canada M4V 3B2
Penguin Books (N.Z.) Ltd, 182–190 Wairau Road, Auckland 10, New Zealand
Penguin Books Ltd, Registered Offices: Harmondsworth, Middlesex, England

Originally published in hardcover by
Dial Books for Young Readers
A Division of Penguin Books USA Inc.

The art for this book was prepared by using watercolors. It was
then color-separated and reproduced in red, yellow, blue, and
black halftones.

GOING TO SLEEP ON THE FARM
is also available in hardcover from
Dial Books for Young Readers.

How does a cow go to sleep—tell me how?
How does a cow go to sleep?

A cow lies down in the soft, sweet hay,

in a cozy barn, at the end of day.

And that's how a cow goes to sleep—Moo-moo.
That's how a cow goes to sleep.

How does a duck go to sleep—tell me how?
How does a duck go to sleep?

A duck tucks his bill right under his wing,

and doesn't worry about a thing.

And that's how a duck goes to sleep—Quack, quack.
That's how a duck goes to sleep.

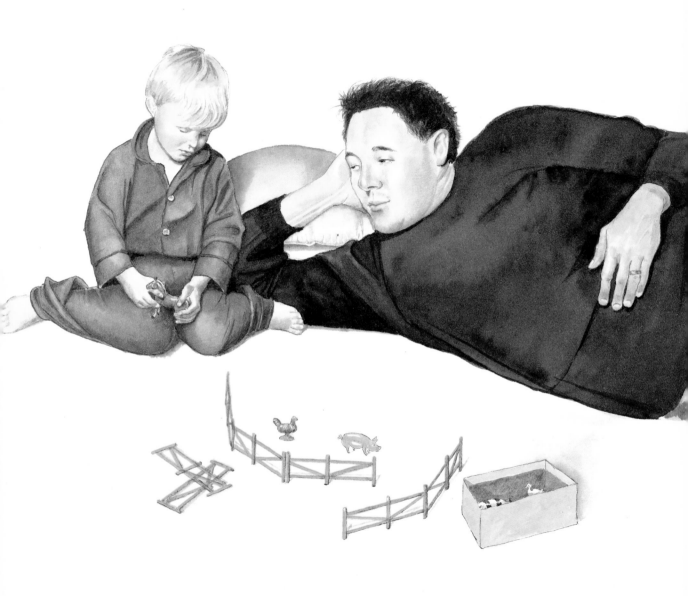

How does a horse go to sleep—tell me how?
How does a horse go to sleep?

A horse, of course, stands up all night,

while he's fast asleep, with his eyes shut tight.

And that's how a horse goes to sleep—Neighh-h-h.
That's how a horse goes to sleep.

How does a pig go to sleep—tell me how?
How does a pig go to sleep?

A pig curls up with her family or friends.

Where one pig starts, another pig ends.

And that's how a pig goes to sleep—Oink, oink.
That's how a pig goes to sleep.

How does a hen go to sleep—tell me how?
How does a hen go to sleep?

A hen fluffs her feathers so they look their best,

and sits on her eggs, all warm in her nest.

And that's how a hen goes to sleep—Cluck, cluck.
That's how a hen goes to sleep.

How do you go to sleep—tell me how?
How do you go to sleep?

You snuggle down in your nice warm bed,
And sleepy dreams soon fill your head.

And that's how you go to sleep—Shh-h-h.
That's how you go to sleep.

Wendy Cheyette Lewison

was born in Brooklyn, New York. She has written many books for children, including the recently published Dial title *The Rooster Who Lost His Crow*. A member of the Authors Guild, Ms. Lewison has taught kindergarten, edited children's books, and worked in a children's bookstore. She lives in Westchester, New York, with her husband and two children.

Juan Wijngaard

studied art at the Royal College of Art in England and has won several major awards for his illustrations. His most recent book published by Dial, *Thunderstorm!* by Nathaniel Tripp, received a starred review from *School Library Journal,* which praised his "exquisite watercolors [that] dramatically portray the sequence of the storm's approach." Mr. Wijngaard now lives in Santa Monica, California, with his wife and son.